1989

Laura Beth Terry
Happy Birthday
From Gia + Gina Roell

# Walt Disney

# Snow White
## and the
# Seven Dwarfs

Twin Books

GALLERY BOOKS
An imprint of W.H. Smith Publishers Inc.
112 Madison Avenue
New York, New York 10016

Once upon a time, in a far away castle, a princess was born on a winter's night. Her skin was as white as the falling snow, and her mother, the Queen, named her Snow White. As the years passed, she grew into a lovely child. Her gentle nature won the hearts of all.

One day, the Queen became ill and died. After a time of sadness, the King remarried. The new Queen was very beautiful, but also jealous and mean. She forced Snow White to dress in rags and to scrub the castle floors on her hands and knees. Snow White obeyed without complaint.

Each morning, the proud Queen stood before her magic mirror and demanded: "Mirror, mirror, on the wall, Who is the fairest one of all?"

"You, O Queen, are the fairest in the land," the mirror would reply.

Then the vain Queen smiled with pleasure.

However, Snow White was growing up, and ragged clothes could not hide her beauty.

Snow White was unaware of her stepmother's jealousy. She carried out her work with a smile, and when she could, she daydreamed to escape her dreary life. She dreamed that one day a charming prince would arrive on a white horse and carry her off to his palace.

One morning, as she drew water from the well, her friends the doves whispered to her. "This is a magic well. Tell it your wishes and they will come true."

Snow White looked into the well and murmured, "I wish that my prince would come."

No sooner had she spoken these words than a handsome young Prince appeared at her side. "Princess, you are even more beautiful than in my dreams. Will you be mine?" he asked.

"Oh, yes!" replied Snow White. "I was waiting for you."

The Prince came to see her every day at the same hour.

There beside the well they made plans. "I shall ask the King, your father, if we can be married," said Prince Charming.

"Yes, but my stepmother is very strict. She might tell him to refuse," said Snow White with a sigh. When it was time for Prince Charming to leave, Snow White waved goodbye from her balcony.

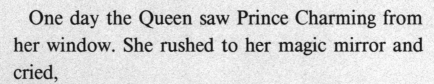

One day the Queen saw Prince Charming from her window. She rushed to her magic mirror and cried,
"Mirror, mirror, on the wall,
Who is the fairest one of all?"

The mirror replied:
"Her lips blood red,
Her hair like night,
Her skin like snow,
Her name—Snow White!"

The Queen was furious. She summoned her huntsman. "Snow White has made me very angry! Tomorrow at dawn, take her deep into the forest. I want you to kill her and bring back her heart in this golden casket. This will prove that you have obeyed me."

The next morning the huntsman invited Snow White to take a walk in the forest. Snow White was delighted to have a rest from her daily work.

"Perhaps the Queen likes me after all," she said. "I shall bring her a bouquet of flowers."

Off into the forest they went. Snow White picked flowers while the huntsman watched at a distance.

The huntsman followed the Queen's orders and let Snow White roam far into the forest. When she sat down to catch her breath, a tiny bird came and perched on her finger. All the animals knew and loved Snow White.

Suddenly, the huntsman stood over her.

"Is it time to go back?" she asked. The huntsman did not answer.

"What's wrong?" she asked.

"I'm afraid you won't be going back," he said, with tears in his eyes.

Snow White jumped to her feet. "What do you mean?" she cried in alarm.

The huntsman fell to his knees, sobbing. "I can't do it!" he cried, and then told the Princess what the Queen had ordered. "Please forgive me for having accepted this horrible task. I'd rather die myself than harm you."

Snow White was no longer afraid. She knew that this man would not hurt her. "But your life will be in danger if you return with an empty casket," she said.

The huntsman raised his head and said, "You must run away and hide in the forest. I shall kill a deer and put its heart into the casket. The Queen will never know the difference. We will both be safe."

There was no time to lose. Snow White thanked the
huntsman for sparing her life, and ran off into the
forest. Her heart beat loudly as she rushed and stumbled
through the woods. The farther she ran, the darker it
became. It seemed as if even the trees were trying to
reach out and grab her.

"Where shall I go? Where shall I hide?" she cried as
she fled deeper into the woods.

Faster and faster she ran, until she could run no
farther. Falling to the ground, she burst into tears. She
thought of the castle that was so far away. And the
Prince. What would happen when he went to meet her
at the well tomorrow? "He'll look for me, and if he
doesn't find me, he'll go away forever," she sobbed.

Just then, she heard a noise and looked up. All
around her were hundreds of tiny blinking lights. They
were the eyes of the little forest creatures. They had
come to help their friend.

"Don't cry, Snow White," said the little deer, "we'll take care of you."

Snow White sat up and wiped away her tears. "Oh, if only you knew what's happened..."

"But we do know!" cried the rabbits, chipmunks and squirrels. "News travels fast in the forest!"

"I must find someplace to hide. I can't keep running forever," said the tired Princess.

All the animals began chattering at once. Each one had a suggestion.

"We'll hide you in our nest," chirped the birds.

"No, she can live with us," said the raccoons, tugging at her skirt.

Everyone wanted to be helpful, but a Princess can hardly live in a nest or a hole in the ground. Finally it was the deer who had the best suggestion. "There's a little house nearby. You can live there."

"Why, of course. The little house!" shouted the other animals. "Quick! Follow us, we'll show you the way." And before she could say a word, Snow White found herself being led away by the animals.

The birds were the first to arrive. When Snow White pushed aside the branches, she clapped her hands in joy. "What an adorable little house! So tiny and cozy. Who lives there?"

Instead of answering, the animals gently nudged her on.

She crept up to the door and knocked. There was no answer. "Perhaps I'll just take a peek inside," she said, as she opened the door.

"Oh, my!" she exclaimed as she stepped into the house. "The children who live here certainly have no one to look after them. Look at all the cobwebs and dust. Now that I'm here, perhaps I'll just tidy up a bit."

And soon, not only Snow White, but the animals too, were busy dusting and sweeping. The rabbit held the dustpan, while the squirrels unraveled cobwebs and dusted the shelves with their bushy tails.

When all was neat and clean downstairs, Snow White decided to have a look in the room above.

It was beginning to grow dark, so Snow White lit a candle. She then followed her little helpers up the stairs. There she found seven small beds all lined up in a row. A name was written on each of the beds: Happy, Dopey, Grumpy, Sneezy, Sleepy, Bashful and Doc.

"What funny names these children have," said Snow White. "Sleepy..." she yawned. "I'm feeling a bit sleepy myself. Perhaps I'll take a short nap..." And before she could finish her sentence, she was fast asleep.

The animals crept out, leaving the tired Princess to have her rest.

In the meantime, in a nearby mine, seven little men were finishing up their day's work. They were the dwarfs who lived in the little house in the forest.

Every morning they would leave their home to go and search for diamonds in a tunnel that they had dug deep inside the mountain.

Day after day, they set out at dawn, singing as they went: "Heigh-Ho! Heigh-Ho! It's off to work we go! We keep on singing all day long with a Heigh! Heigh-Ho!"

Now it was time to lay down their picks and shovels and head home.

"Wait a minute!" shouted Doc. "I think I've found something!" He pushed back his glasses and looked through his special magnifying glass.

The other dwarfs held their breaths. It was not often that they found a real diamond.

"Perfect!" Doc cried at last. "Now we can go home and celebrate!"

The dwarfs slung their picks over their shoulders and marched off in a line. They began to sing as they marched:

"Heigh-Ho! Heigh-Ho! It's home from work we go. We keep on singing all night long with a Heigh! Heigh-Ho!"

Doc led the way with a lantern. Behind him was Grumpy, then Happy, Sleepy, Sneezy, Bashful and last of all, Dopey. The seven tired and hungry dwarfs looked forward to reaching their snug little home.

All of a sudden Doc stopped in his tracks.

"Whaaaa whaaa ttttss AAHHA CHEWWW! wrong?" asked Sneezy, who always sneezed at the worst moment.

"Look!" said Doc as he pointed toward the house. "There's a light in the window."

"Oh, no! Someone must be there," squeaked Bashful in his tiny voice.

"Oh, boy! A visitor!" cried Happy, who always saw the bright side of things.

"I'm tired. Let's go in," said Sleepy with a yawn.

"Careful," whispered Grumpy, "it might be a robber."

The dwarfs tiptoed up to the house. They slowly pushed the door open, careful not to make a sound. Seven heads peeked into the room.

They were speechless. Never had they seen their home looking so spotless. They could hardly believe their eyes! Grumpy was the first to speak. "Who dared to wash my shirt?"

"And look at my bowl!" protested Sneezy.

"What nerve! To walk into someone's house and create a revolution!" declared Doc, who liked to use big words.

"Yes… but a nice revolution!" said Bashful shyly.

"Hum!" mumbled Grumpy, "we'd better find the person who did this."

"We should look upstairs," said Sleepy, who was worried about his bed.

The dwarfs crept up the stairs, ready for battle. Entering the bedroom, they saw a large form spread across their beds.

"Whoever it is, he's fast asleep," whispered Doc.

"Hum! I've a thing or two to say to that robber when he wakes up!" said Grumpy.

"But nothing was stolen," said Bashful.

"I don't care," said Sleepy, "I want my bed back!"

"Shush! It's moving," whispered Doc.

And what did these brave little men do? They ran and hid at the foot of the beds!

Sure enough, the form was moving. It stretched out its arms and yawned.

The dwarfs kept still. No one dared to move an inch. But Sneezy could not control himself. "AH AH AH CHEEWW!" This enormous sneeze was enough to wake anyone.

And that's exactly what happened. Snow White sat up.

Happy was the first to speak. "A girl!" he said, and he began to laugh. "Our robber is a girl!"

Snow White began to giggle. "And I thought that you were children." Everyone began to laugh at this. Everyone, that is, except Grumpy, who scowled in the background.

"Oh! Excuse me. I ought to introduce myself. My name is Snow White. I've come here to escape my stepmother…" She then told the dwarfs about her adventure in the forest.

When she had finished her tale, the dwarfs became very excited.

"Don't worry, Snow White. You can stay here with us. We'll protect you from the wicked Queen," declared Doc. The other dwarfs nodded their heads in agreement. All except Grumpy.

"Not so fast!" said Grumpy in his gruff voice. "We should think about this."

"There's nothing to think about," replied Doc. "The Princess will stay with us!"

"Hurrah!" shouted the dwarfs, tossing their caps in the air.

In the meantime, in her
room in the castle, the
Queen looked into her magic
mirror and asked,
"Mirror, mirror, on the wall,
Now who is the fairest one
of all?"
   The faithful mirror replied,
   "Over the seven jeweled
hills,
Beyond the seventh fall,
In the cottage of the seven
dwarfs,
Dwells Snow White,
The fairest one of all."
   "I've been tricked!"
screamed the Queen.
"Someone shall pay for this!"
She grabbed the casket
containing the doe's heart
and threw it to the ground.

High up in the castle tower, the Queen prepared a magic potion to change her so that Snow White would not recognize her.

"Just this very last ingredient and all will be ready," she said to the raven who watched from above.

The potion worked! The Queen was transformed. She had lost her teeth and her nose was long and crooked. She had become an ugly old witch! "Ha! Ha! Now my little Snow White, I'm going to prepare a special treat for you," cackled the old witch. "First I'll take this juicy red apple and dip it into the poison."

The witch lowered the apple into a steaming, boiling pot. "One bite of this fruit and she'll be dead. Then we'll see who is the most beautiful woman in the kingdom," hissed the wicked Queen.

It was dinner time at the dwarfs' house. Seven hungry little men rushed toward the table.

"Wait a minute," said Snow White. "First show me your hands."

"I knew there'd be trouble," mumbled Grumpy, as the dwarfs looked at each other in surprise.

"Now! Now!" said Snow White softly. "Let's have a look at those hands."

One by one the dwarfs held out their hands.

"Oh dear! Look at those grubby hands and dirty fingernails. No one sits down at the table with hands like those. A little soap and water should do the trick. Off you go!" she said, pointing toward the wash basin.

The dwarfs meekly went
out and began to wash. All,
that is, except Grumpy.

"I knew it! Now look what
she's done. Princess or
not—no one's going to tell
me what to do!" he declared.

"Oh Grumpy! You're
always complaining. It
doesn't hurt to wash once in
a while," said the others.
"And being such good
friends we'll even help you!"
And so Grumpy received a
good scrub!

Later that evening the dwarfs took out their instruments. They were going to have a party for Snow White.

The dwarfs took turns dancing with Snow White. Dopey decided to surprise the Princess. Grabbing a long cloak, he climbed onto Sneezy's shoulders. Now he was as tall as the Princess!

"Why, who's this dashing young man?" asked Snow White, as she began to dance. Suddenly, she thought of Prince Charming and became sad.

"Don't be sad." said Happy. "I'm sure your prince is looking for you. Don't worry, he'll find you."

And with this joyful thought the party continued.

That night, while Snow White and the dwarfs slept peacefully in their beds, the wicked Queen left the castle by way of the moat that separated it from the forest. An evil gleam flashed in her eyes as she rowed toward the forest's edge. A basket of shiny red apples lay at her feet.

The next day, before setting off for work, the seven dwarfs lined up for an inspection. Snow White looked at their hands and faces and rewarded each dwarf with a kiss.

"Bashful, you are so handsome when your face is clean," said Snow White as she bent down to give him a kiss on the top of his shiny head. Bashful blushed with pleasure.

"Next!"

When the dwarfs had gone, Snow White began
to prepare a special treat. "I'm going to bake a
pie," she told her animal friends, who'd come
to visit.

"Lucky dwarfs!" said the chipmunk, smacking
his lips and rubbing his tummy. Then footsteps
were heard approaching the house.

"Who could that be?" Snow White asked her
friends.

An old woman
appeared at the window.
She looked so ragged and
poor that Snow White
felt sorry for her.

"Good morning. What
can I do for you?"
inquired Snow White
gently.

The old woman took
an apple and handed it
to Snow White. "I can
see that you are very
kind," she said. "Here,
take this lovely red apple.
It's a present."

The animals who were watching from outside began to panic. They knew that the old woman was really the wicked Queen. "Quick!" cried the squirrel. "We must go and tell the dwarfs before it's too late!" Snow White was about to take a bite.

There was no time for long explanations! The animals ran like the wind to where the dwarfs were working. The deer grabbed Bashful by the seat of his pants. "Hey! What's going on?" cried the poor little dwarf, turning as red as a beet.

"Hurry! Hurry!" cried the birds. "Snow White... wicked Queen... poison apple... danger!"

This was all that the dwarfs needed to hear. Off they went as fast as their little legs could carry them.

It was too late! Snow White had eaten part of the apple. She felt dizzy, the room began to whirl, and she fell to the floor.

"Aha!" the wicked witch cackled with glee. "So, my pretty little Princess. Did you enjoy your apple? Ha, ha, ha!" The old woman's evil laugh echoed throughout the little house.

"Now I will return to the castle. My magic mirror will tell me the truth. We'll see who's the fairest one of all!" said the wicked Queen, as she rushed out into the forest.

The dwarfs rushed toward their house, riding on the backs of the deer.

"There she is! There's the wicked Queen!" cried the birds.

"Follow her!" shouted Grumpy, waving a big stick.

The witch saw the dwarfs and ran off in the other direction. The magic potion enabled her to run even faster than the deer.

"Faster! Faster!" yelled the rabbit. "Don't let her get away!"

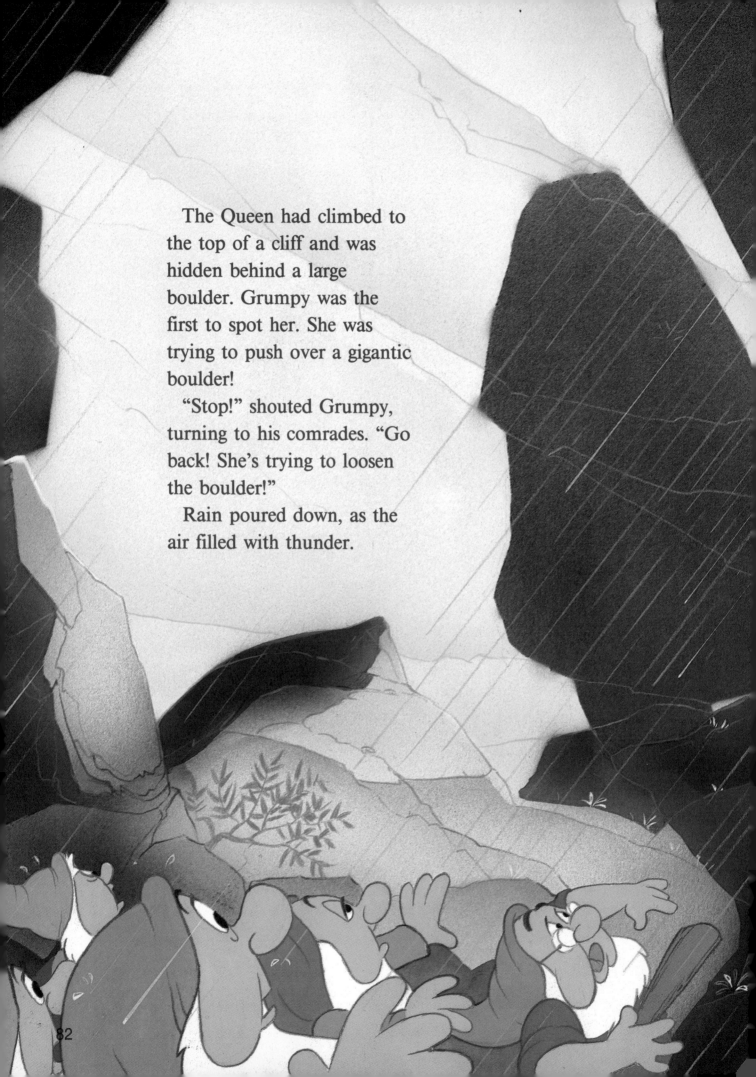

The Queen had climbed to
the top of a cliff and was
hidden behind a large
boulder. Grumpy was the
first to spot her. She was
trying to push over a gigantic
boulder!

"Stop!" shouted Grumpy,
turning to his comrades. "Go
back! She's trying to loosen
the boulder!"

Rain poured down, as the
air filled with thunder.

The enormous stone had begun to move.
A loud crack was heard as a tremendous bolt of
lightning split the air. The witch, startled by the
thunder, lost her balance and fell backward into
the dark abyss.

When the next flash lit up the sky, the rock
was still there, but the wicked Queen had
disappeared forever!

When the weary dwarfs returned to the house, they found Snow White lying on the floor. They gently lifted her up and placed her on her bed. Tears streamed down their faces as they knelt beside their beloved Snow White.

The dwarfs built a special coffin for Snow White. It was made of crystal, so that they could always see her lovely face.

They placed her outside in the middle of the woods, where all her animal friends could see her too. Day after day, the dwarfs visited her, each one wishing deep in his heart that she would wake up.

Soon spring arrived. Flowers blossomed around Snow White's tomb.

One day, as the dwarfs knelt in the forest, they heard the sound of hoofbeats. It was a handsome young man on a white horse.

"It's Prince Charming," whispered the animals. "He's been looking everywhere for the Princess."

The Prince jumped off his horse and ran to the coffin. Slowly, he lifted the crystal lid.

"How lovely she is!" exclaimed Prince Charming as he looked at her face. Leaning closer, he gently kissed her pale lips.

Suddenly, Snow White's eyelids began to flutter. A smile spread slowly across her lips. She opened her eyes.

"My Prince has come," she murmured softly.

Prince Charming led Snow White away on his white
horse. In his palace high on a hill, they lived happily
ever after as King and Queen of the land.

Produced by
Twin Books
15 Sherwood Place
Greenwich, CT. 06830.

ISBN 0-8317-7885-7

Published by Gallery Books
A Division of W.H. Smith Publishers Inc.
112 Madison Avenue
New York, New York 10016.

Copyright © 1986 The Walt Disney Company.

Printed in Hong Kong

3 4 5 6 7 8 9 10

The Prince gathered Snow White into his arms. Shouts of joy rang out around them. The dwarfs hugged each other with delight.

Snow White was alive!

The Princess looked down at her little friends. "I must leave you now to go away with my Prince. But I will never forget you. You will always be in my heart."